Triston

have Best wishes!
XOXO love Natalie

ns!

He will be amazing! Cooper

Raygyn

Best wishes!
Emily

Eliot

Ethan

Danny

hope you give
him hug's and kisses
xoxo Mckinley

Happy
Reading
♡ Mrs.
Smith

If WAFFLES

Were Like

BOYS

CHARISE MERICLE HARPER

ILLUSTRATED BY
SCOTT MAGOON

Balzer + Bray
An Imprint of HarperCollins Publishers

Balzer + Bray is an imprint of HarperCollins Publishers.

If Waffles Were Like Boys
Text copyright © 2011 by Charise Mericle Harper
Illustrations copyright © 2011 by Scott Magoon
All rights reserved. Manufactured in China.

Library of Congress Cataloging-in-Publication Data is available.
ISBN 978-0-06-177998-5 (trade bdg.) — ISBN 978-0-06-177999-2 (lib. bdg.)

Typography by Carla Weise
11 12 13 14 15 SCP 10 9 8 7 6 5 4 3 2 1
❖
First Edition

For Luther, my favorite boy!
—C.M.H.

For Owen, Daniel, Drew & Jack.
Let's have waffles together sometime.
—S.M.

If waffles were like boys . . .

If socks were like boys . . .

laundry baskets would
be **PIRATE SHIPS!**

If shopping carts were like boys . . .

If hot dogs were like boys . . .

picnics would be
RODEOS!

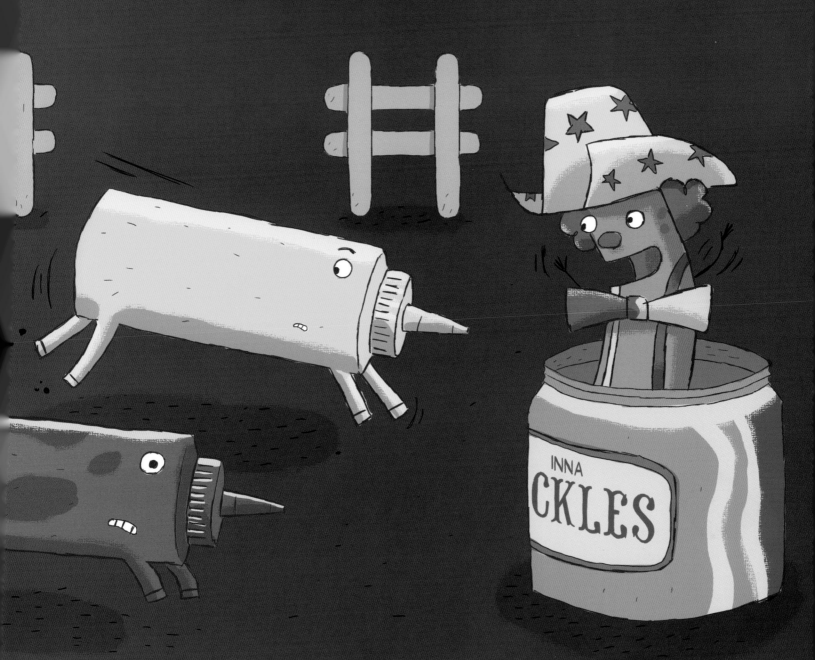

If cars were like boys . . .

If peas were like boys . . .

dinner plates would be PLAYGROUNDS!

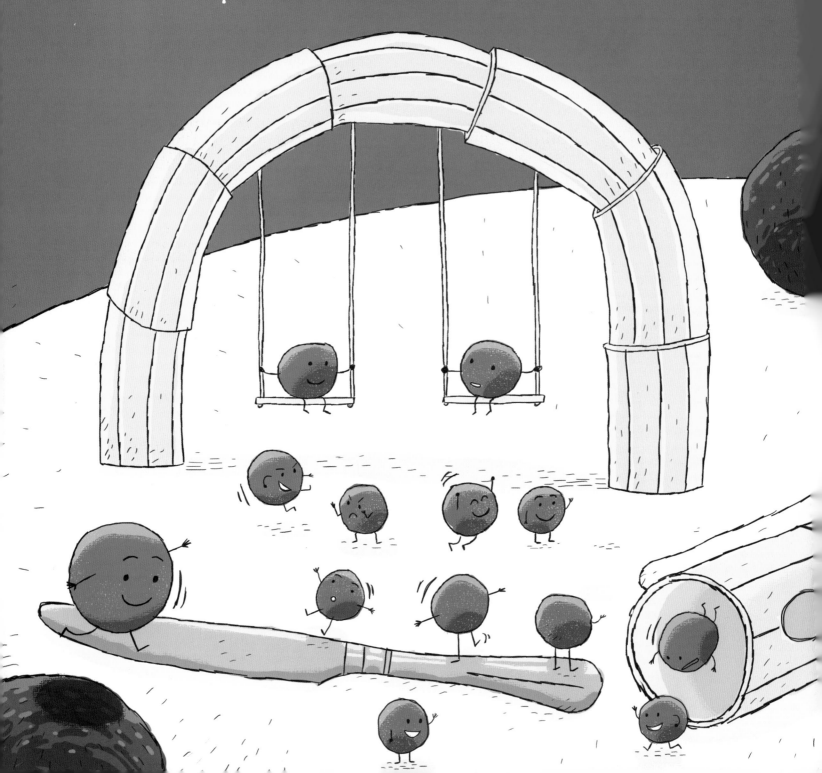

If toothbrushes were like boys . . .

If pillows were like boys . . .

If stars were like boys . . .

night skies would be
FIREWORKS!

Good night, boys.